CW00401201

A Chief Inspector Blc

# The

# Mystery

# At

# Wentworth

# Park

*by*

# Ann Sutton

Published by

Wild Poppy Publishing LLC
Highland, UT 84003


Distributed by Wild Poppy Publishing


Cover design by Julie Matern
Cover Design ©2022 Wild Poppy Publishing LLC

*Dedicated to*

Rae Sutton

# Style Note

I am a naturalized American citizen born and raised in the United Kingdom. I have readers in America, the UK, Australia, Canada and beyond. But my book is set in the United Kingdom.

So which version of English should I choose?

I chose American English as it is my biggest audience, my family learns this English and my editor suggested it was the most logical.

This leads to criticism from those in other English-speaking countries, but I have neither the time nor the resources to do a special edition for each country.

I do use British words, phrases and idioms whenever I can (unless my editor does not understand them and then it behooves me to change it so that it is not confusing to my readers).

Previously published as *Mystery at Wentworth Park, Episodes 1-11* on Kindle Vella.

**Dodo Dorchester meets the brooding Chief Inspector Blood in 'Murder at Farrington Hall' and again in 'Murder at the Races' and sparks fly. But it is 1923, and though things have changed since the Great War, a romance between an earl's daughter and a policeman is out of the question. In this novella, learn how Blood truly feels about Dodo and whether he will ever find love.**

Now available as an eBook, *Mystery at Wentworth Park.*

# Table of Contents

# Prologue

Chief Inspector Blood stared after her, watching as that overly nice Charlie put an arm around her. His chest ached as she tipped her head to rest on the young man's shoulder.

Though a tragedy had just unfolded, he only had energy for the morass of emotions currently trying to break out of his chest. Emotions that had exploded through him as her hair had touched his chin in the tight quarters of the broom closet and her honeyed breath brushed his skin.

"Chief Inspector, should I alert the hospital staff?" The words of the constable seemed distant, disconnected from reality; the reality that he had developed deep, forbidden feelings for the Honorable Lady Dorothea Dorchester.

"Yes."

Had he really answered, or did he just imagine answering? Nothing else mattered. Only the truth that she inspired feelings in him he had never felt before. Feelings that he could never confess to or act on.

The temptation to kiss her in the closet while the mad woman raged outside had been almost too strong to resist.

Almost.

Had she felt it too?

How long he stood in a vortex of jealousy watching them, he did not know. Constables ran around him like ants, recording the details of the suicide from the roof of St Thomas' hospital as he remained rooted in disappointment.

# Chapter 1

Benedict Blood had joined the police force because he felt it was his calling. He also had a bent for method and order. Police work satisfied both these inclinations.

Starting as a regular bobby with a beat on the streets of Westminster, he had worn the uniform of a constable with honor and pride and risen quickly in the ranks. At the expense of any kind of social life.

The police force was his mistress. All his time, talents and energies were devoted to it and the reward she gave him was promotion. He became the youngest inspector in the organization's history, going on to become a chief inspector before his thirtieth birthday.

Only one thing had interrupted his upward progression - the Great War. Called up in 1915 at the age of twenty-four, he had seen things that had changed him, things no man should ever have to see. He locked those nightmare memories away and sealed them with a key. However, his service had prepared him to deal with murder. He was rarely shocked by a case.

It had also sobered him as a person.

Never the life and soul of any party, since the War he had become serious, contemplative and, he had heard, distant. That is until meeting Dodo. Though there was no future for him with a woman like her, Dodo Dorchester had sparked something in him he believed had died. She had stirred his soul back to life.

Over the years he had disciplined himself to suppress any attraction to women he met on the job. His career was not kind to relationships; he traveled extensively and kept horrible hours. It was no life for a wife. And the things he witnessed made him sour at times; not a good quality in a companion.

But Dodo managed to penetrate his armor—immediately. There was something about her that grabbed him by the scruff of the neck and wouldn't let go. His defense was to be boorish and gruff. He had growled at her like the stereotypical bull of a policeman whose pride has been put out of joint.

Instead of gracefully bowing out, this feisty young woman had rippled with suppressed anger and dug in her heels. He had admired her for it.

He had also purposefully offended her.

Which he had hoped would make her back off and keep his life simple.

Instead, it had emboldened her.

To make matters worse, Sir Matthew Cusworth had called to suggest that he include her in the investigation.

Thus, began his torture.

# Chapter 2

Benedict Blood never took a day off.

But after the Ascot case closed, he broke with precedent and took three full days leave, giving some cock and bull story about an aunt dying so that no one would question him. He needed time; time for his heart to heal. He loved Dodo but she was out of reach. He needed to move on. Forget her.

His mother, Martha, was still living in Southwark, south of the river, a widow with only one child still at home: Terry, his special brother.

As soon as he showed up on her doorstep, his mother knew something was wrong.

"Benny," she cried, throwing her arms around him. "To what do I owe this honor?" Her smile was too bright, and the anxiety in her eyes did not match the curve of her mouth.

"Can't a man come to see his own mother without raising eyebrows?" he joked, but his voice was off.

He walked across the tiny room to the wheelchair containing his brother and wrapped him in a bear hug. He could feel his mother's eyes boring into his back.

"I'll put the kettle on," she said, and wandered into the minuscule kitchen.

He sat by his brother. Blood could be his true self with Terry, who never asked awkward questions. Terry just smiled and made Benedict feel like he was the only person in Terry's world.

Blood had no regrets about going without so that he could purchase the wheelchair for Terry. Nor about his humble bachelor flat that looked out onto a brick wall, so that he could install his mother in this ground floor apartment. Here his mother could take Terry out for long walks along the embankment without having to navigate any stairs.

His mother returned, wiping her hands on her scrupulously clean apron. "How have you been, love?"

"I just wrapped up a big case. You might have read about it?"

"The one involving the MP? I saw your name in the paper." Pride was an insufficient word to describe the sparkle in his mother's chocolate brown eyes. "Who would think a member of parliament would have such a dark secret?"

He huffed. "You'd be surprised at the secrets people have, Mum."

"And what are you doing here on a Wednesday at two in the afternoon? Not that we don't love to see you. We do, don't we Terry?" Terry jerked his head in assent, beaming from ear to ear.

"It was time for a break. I haven't had a day off in four years." His gaze darted around the room, resting on his mother's anxious face for just a second.

She pursed her lips and nodded without saying a word. He was grateful.

The kettle whistled and his mother disappeared into the tiny kitchen again.

"I thought we could take Terry out," he suggested. "It's a lovely day."

"We haven't been out for our constitutional yet, have we, Terry? Let's all go after we've finished our tea."

Blood looked around the cramped room, dotted with photographs of his brothers and sisters amid old coronation memorabilia. A large picture of his deceased father occupied pride of place on the small fireplace.

"Here we are." His mother pushed into the room holding a tray. Blood jumped up to help.

"Sit down, son. When I can't do this by myself, it's time to check out."

He smiled at her fierce independence, watching as she poured him a steaming cup and added two sugars and milk.

"There now." She handed him the cup. "Just how you like it."

He took a sip and memories of childhood crashed about in his brain; reading from a pile of used books his parents scrimped to buy, winning the scholarship at the local grammar school, playing with his brothers and sisters in their old house.

His mother poured a little tea for Terry and moved to help him.

"Let me do it, Mum," he said, intercepting her and taking the cup. He scooted closer to his brother and gently tipped the cup against his mouth. In his excitement, Terry waved his arms and knocked a little of the warm, sweet liquid out of his mouth. Blood took out a handkerchief and gently wiped Terry's chin.

The whole family, including himself when he wasn't in the middle of a case, gathered in that tiny flat for Sunday dinner. His mother would roast four chickens and divide them between the sixteen of them, which included several grandchildren. There were far too many of them to eat around a table, so they all sat with plates on their knees, elbow to elbow, and then strolled along the river when the weather was fine. The only interruption to this ritual had been during the war when three, then four of Martha Blood's sons were conscripted into the army. All but one had come home.

Every member of his family contributed a little so that their mother could spend all her time with Terry and not have to work. A doctor had once suggested that he be placed in a public nursing facility. He had regretted the words as soon as they were out of his mouth due to the tongue-lashing Martha had given him.

All his brothers worked at the docks like their father and his sisters' husbands were dockhands too. The River Thames was the lifeblood of the Blood family.

After helping wash the cups, they rolled Terry through the door and started on their stroll. Blood could have navigated the route with his eyes closed.

The pigeons and gulls swooped, and Terry hooted with his own brand of laughter.

Pointing to a bench, his mother said, "Let's sit down and enjoy the sun. It will do Terry good. It's the first bright day this week."

Blood positioned the wheelchair and they sat in companionable silence watching the boats and the birds, breathing in the familiar smells. It was one of the things he loved about his mother—she never pried. But he had come to seek her advice and now was as good a time as any.

"I met a girl."

No cry, no change in position, no hands thrown in the air. "A girl? What is she like?" Martha Blood kept her eyes firmly on the water.

"She is beautiful, intelligent, funny…and the daughter of an earl."

"Ah." The single exclamation was loaded with a million nuances.

He threw a pebble into the water. "I've never felt this way. Never wanted to feel this way."

Martha clasped her work-worn hands. "Does she know?"

"If you mean, have I told her? No. If you mean, does she feel the same way? I think so."

His mother rocked the wheelchair back and forth as if it were a pram, as Terry nodded his head and smiled.

Blood picked up another rock. "Of course, it can't come to anything."

The cry of a lone gull pierced the silence.

"Of course," she finally said, nodding.

Benedict grabbed the hat from his head and turned it in his hands. "But she has made me feel…alive."

A full five minutes passed as they watched a cargo boat work its way by. Terry waved.

The hat stilled. "I wanted to kiss her more than I have ever wanted anything in my life."

Out of the corner of his eye he could see his mother frown. "Did you?"

"No." *But I wish I had.*

His mother's dry, cracked hand reached out and covered his own. "Perhaps she's shown you that the time is right, love. You've been so devoted to your work that you've ignored your personal life. It's not good for a man to be alone."

"This is no life for a wife, Mum."

"Nonsense! It is a respected profession, with a decent wage and good standing in the community." She touched her finger to his cheek. "And you should not waste that bonny face."

He chuckled.

"If she loves you, a woman will make any sacrifice. You just need to find the right one, son. And you already know, this earl's daughter, she's not the right one."

They sat for a long time each lost in their thoughts.

As they made the walk back to his mother's home, his heart squeezing in his chest, Blood made a decision. He would take time to heal and then knock down the emotional wall.

It was time to find *the one*.

# Chapter 3

## Six Months Later

On a Monday morning, Blood's commanding officer sent for him.

*This office has enjoyed a lick of paint in the last few years, unlike mine.*

"You called for me sir?" Blood stretched to his full, six foot two.

The commander looked up from the pile of papers on his desk. "Yes, we have a tricky case and I think you are the man for the job."

It had been some time since Blood had caught a case he could really sink his teeth into, and he was more than ready.

The commander lifted his chin. "Lady Monroe-Spencer's dog has been kidnapped."

Blood frowned in cold silence.

His boss tipped his head to the side. "I know you're used to murders, Blood, but this family is extremely high profile. Her husband is on a hush-hush steering committee in the current government and the higher-ups are concerned that this may be a threat. A warning if you like. If someone is targeting Lord Monroe-Spencer, we would like to catch them before they succeed."

Blood rolled his shoulders.

"Your work with the upper classes has not gone unnoticed," the commander continued. "You were requested for this assignment by the Prime Minister himself." He raised his brows waiting for Blood's reaction.

*The Prime Minister!*

The indignity he initially felt rolled off. If he made a name for himself with this case, he would be on the fast track for another promotion.

"And you can take that friend of yours, Lady Dorothea. She has a way with handling her set."

The balloon of pride that had been filling fizzled into a heap on the floor.

"That will not be possible, sir." A strange twisting in his chest made it difficult to breathe.

"Oh?" The commanding officer had stopped looking at the paperwork on his desk and was leveling his gaze at Blood.

"I believe she is abroad at the present time."

He tried not to care, but when he came upon a society magazine, he would flick through the pages hoping for a glimpse. It was his guilty pleasure. Last week he had seen a picture of Dodo headed to the Mediterranean. She was laughing, her whole face alight as she held a glass of champagne. The article said she would be gone for a month.

"Ah, well then. I hope you've learned a thing or two about treading lightly." The false smile on the commander's face indicated doubt.

"I will do my best, sir."

The commander handed him the file. "You should leave on the twelve-fifteen train. The locals are waiting and will meet you at the station." He ran a hand down his uniform. "Keep me in the loop, Blood. There are a lot of people watching this."

Ж

As a chief inspector, Blood was permitted to travel second class but even those carriages were full today and he had spent an uncomfortable two hours, crushed into a tight compartment with several people including a mother with two young children who had spent the better part of the journey poking their tongues out at him. He had suppressed an urge to poke out his own.

It was raining outside, and the damp coats of the passengers had fogged up the windows making it impossible to see the countryside they were passing on their way to Sussex county.

In the end, he had tipped his trilby over his eyes and tried to nap.

As the train pulled into the station, he jerked awake, slipped his hat back, and gathered his things. Stepping out onto the platform he was pleased to see that the weather here was brighter than in London. He shrugged off his raincoat and hung it over his arm.

A man in the unmistakable uniform of a cheap, wrinkled suit, scuffed shoes and a light coat, moved forward, hand extended.

"Good afternoon, sir." They shook hands. "Inspector Bridger at your service." The man was well over forty with salt and pepper hair that grazed his collar. "Welcome to Budleigh-Milton, Chief Inspector."

Blood nodded. "Thank you, Bridger. Now let's get cracking." They moved to leave the small station that was hung with baskets of bright annuals. "I've read the file but would like to hear your take on things."

"This way then, sir."

An older, black Ford was waiting, with a driver. Inspector Bridger held open the door and Blood slid in.

"The Monroe-Spencer's live in a huge pile three miles into the country. I say *pile* but it is really the pride of the county. It actually comes through Lady Monroe-Spencer's line as Lord Monroe-Spencer lost his estate after the war." Inspector Bridger took out a cigarette case. "Do you mind?"

Blood was not a smoker himself but had no objections to others smoking. He shook his head and the inspector continued.

"Tuesday morning the gardener could not find her Ladyship's dog. This was not altogether unusual, so he did not sound the alarm, expecting the pup to appear at some point. However, after several hours with no sign, the gardener began to worry and sent a note to Lady Monroe-Spencer. She's a short, white, fluffy thing—the dog I mean." The inspector's face cracked wide with a smile and Blood couldn't help but join him. "Anyway, they looked all day and into the night and never found her.

"Lady Monroe-Spencer was inconsolable—she was unable to have any children— but his nibs—" Blood raised an eyebrow at this disrespectful slang term for his Lordship. "—I mean, Lord Monroe-Spencer, immediately worried that they had been targeted. There are a lot of people who stand to lose or make money depending on the conclusions of the special committee he heads."

The sun was struggling to come out from behind the clouds and Blood loosened his tie.

"How do they know the dog didn't just wander off?"

"The dog has never done it before…and is rather partial to food. They are sure she would have some back when she got hungry."

Inspector Bridger wound down the window and a welcoming breeze hit Blood's skin.

"Lord Monroe-Spencer, sensing that this might be a tactic to force him to change politics, immediately called the police station and insisted that they involve Scotland Yard." The inspector pushed his hat back and scratched the top of his head. "Bet you thought you had pulled the short straw when you were assigned to a dognapping."

"My first reaction was not good," Blood admitted. "But I held my tongue and I'm glad I did. I think, given the sensitive nature of his Lordship's position in government, there is every possibility that this *is* a targeted attack."

Inspector Bridger led the chief inspector back to the front hall where they were met by the housekeeper, a middle-aged woman with a harsh set to her jaw. Blood had the impression that her face would crack if she smiled.

"If you'll follow me." Her voice was deep and masculine.

The walked through the flagstone entry and up the grand staircase where the house- keeper knocked and waited.

"Come in, Martin!" The high, upper-class accent was cracked with sobs.

As the chief inspector walked in, he was bathed in sunlight from a south facing picture window. The floral scent was almost oppressive, and lace met the eye at every turn.

A plump woman was sitting in a chair, face lined with distress and a soggy handkerchief clasped to her lips. Beside her, a young nurse was dispensing some kind of tonic.

The female he assumed to be Lady Monroe-Spencer, waved the girl away. "I'd better wait on the sleeping draft if I need to speak to the police," she explained.

The nurse looked up from her charge and Blood felt all the air go out of the room.

"Sit over there, Nurse Farthing," said Lady Monroe-Spencer and waved to a chair covered in lace doilies near the window.

Nurse Farthing dipped her comely head, and Blood quite forgot why he was there.

Inspector Bridger cleared his throat. "This is Chief Inspector Blood, m'lady. Come to investigate about poor Mitzi."

At the mention of the dead dog's name the lady started to blubber, and the two men looked away in embarrassment. "Who would do such a thing?"

When she had composed herself, Blood held out his hand. "Chief Inspector Blood, at your service m'lady."

Lady Monroe-Spencer's face was filled with confusion and Blood wondered if they were wasting their time questioning her.

"Can you tell me what happened, beginning with the last time you saw…Mitzi?"

Lady Monroe-Spencer bit her trembling lip. "Monday morning. I sent dear Mitzi out for her walk with the gardener. One of the maids takes her down. Ten o' clock on the dot. Every day." She wiped her eyes. "Wright, the gardener, takes her around the inner gardens and then lets her off the leash for thirty minutes while he does some weeding." She dabbed her mouth. "He went to fetch her but could not find her—" A sob interrupted the narrative. Lady Monroe-Spencer cleared her throat. "All the staff began a thorough search, to no avail. She will be absolutely lost without me." She dabbed at her cheeks, voice cracking. "Do you believe she has been dog-napped?"

Blood scratched his neck. "It is a possibility. Where was she last seen?"

"In the trees behind the potting shed," Lady Monroe-Spencer replied with a sniff.

"I take it that is not where she usually runs?"

"Well yes, but she always comes back." She dabbed her watery eyes again. He had seen people cry less over lost children.

"Did anyone hear her barking?" he asked.

The nurse shifted in her chair and Blood glanced up to see the pretty, red-headed woman, sitting quietly by the window, her face drawn with concern. She seemed to be taking the loss of the dog hard too.

"What do you mean?" asked lady Monroe-Spencer.

"I mean, that if a stranger took her, might she not have barked?"

Lady Monroe's face flushed crimson. "Are you suggesting that one of the staff did this?"

"I am not suggesting anything m'lady," he said softly, remembering the advice of his commander. "I am merely gathering facts."

Lady Monroe-Spencer patted her cheeks with the handkerchief. "I don't know. No one has mentioned it."

He made a note to ask the gardener about barking.

"Have there been any strangers around the house recently? A painter, or handyman?" He glanced at Nurse Farthing who shrugged.

"I don't think so," said Lady Monroe-Spencer, "but you'll have to ask Mrs. Martin."

Her ladyship's emotions were getting in the way of the interview. It was time to leave.

"Before I go, is there anything else unusual that has happened recently. Anything at all?"

A bright green bird in a gold cage in the corner, jumped down from his perch and chirped.

Lady Monroe-Spencer waved the handkerchief around. "My mind is in chaos, Chief Inspector. I have gone over and over the events of the last few days and I can see no reason why anyone would do this. Why would someone take my darling girl? Everyone loved Mitzi. Everyone." The lady dissolved into tears again and the chief inspector tipped his head to Inspector Bridger. They moved toward the door.

Before reaching it, the nurse rushed over. Her light green eyes indicating that she wanted to tell them something.

"Yes?" said Blood, trying not to notice the way her nurse's uniform hugged her curves.

She stepped into the hall with them her brow clouded.

"I didn't like to mention this with her ladyship so upset and I don't know if there is any connection…"

Bridger and Blood exchanged a puzzled look.

"Anything might be important, Nurse Farthing." He softened his face.

"My cat has gone missing too." She looked up, her eyes glinting with concern.

Blood felt the weight of disappointment, but experience told him to be thorough.

"Your cat?"

"Yes. I'm permitted to have a pet since I live here and she disappeared the same day as the dog."

The hair on the back of Blood's neck stood up.

"Why don't you start at the beginning?"

A small cry came through the door and the nurse glanced over her shoulder. "She needs me. I was giving her a tonic to help her sleep when you came. It should work in about twenty minutes and then I can meet you down in the servants' area."

She slipped back into the room.

Nurse Farthing sat at the long servant's dining table across from the two officers. A small smile stole across her face but was quickly replaced with anguish.

"I'm so worried about Sooty," she began. "It's not like her to be gone for so long. If someone took Mitzi, I am afraid that they took Sooty too." She fiddled with the saltshaker.

"Why is that a concern?" asked Blood.

"Because *I* may not have liked the dog, but my cat did. It was an odd relationship, but they seemed to enjoy each other's company. She would often join Mitzi in the trees where they went missing." Her hair was pulled back under the nurse's cap, highlighting the fine lines of her jaw.

"You didn't like the dog?"

"No, and I'm not the only one."

"Oh?" She and Blood locked eyes and he noticed they were a charming shade of green that complimented her auburn hair.

"Wright hated her," she continued, unaware of the effect she was having on him. "He felt it beneath him to have to fuss over her. He was always complaining that she wasn't a proper dog, like an Alsatian or a Labrador."

19

"Do you believe he had something to do with the kidnapping?" asked Blood.

"Oh no!" Nurse Farthing cried. "I didn't mean to suggest that. I just thought you should know that we didn't all feel about the dog the way her ladyship did."

Blood grinned and a slight blush crept to the nurse's creamy cheeks. She dropped her dark lashes and Blood felt his heart skip.

*Steady on, man. She is a potential suspect.*

"I'm ashamed of my feelings now the poor thing is missing," she continued. "But her ladyship spoils the dog something rotten and it's fat as butter. She barks and snaps all the time."

Blood caught on this fact. "She barks all the time?"

"Yes, she's a yappy little thing. Gets on my nerves, though I generally love dogs." She smiled and Blood felt heat in his veins.

*But no one heard the dog bark when it disappeared.*

Nurse Farthing touched her cap and he noticed her long, elegant fingers. "How long have you worked for Lady Monroe-Spencer?" he asked.

"About three years now. She had a slight stroke and her husband thought it best to hire a full-time nurse."

A maid came in carrying some china, bobbed and put them in a china cabinet.

"Are you happy here?" Blood asked the nurse.

"Yes, on the whole. Her ladyship treats me kindly and I am well compensated."

"Do *you* remember anything odd happening recently?"

"No. The only unfortunate thing that has happened in the whole area is the theft of Lady De Courcy's diamonds and that's miles away. Nothing ever happens here. It's a very quiet place." Her delicate eyes swung up at him accompanied by a dimpled smile.

Blood cleared his throat. "Have you mentioned that your cat is missing to the family?"

"Not yet. I was hoping I was wrong and that she would come back this morning, but she didn't. What I cannot figure out is why anyone would kidnap a dog and a cat."

"It is usually for money. And there is plenty of it here. I take it there has been no ransom note or call?"

"No. And her ladyship may have money, but I certainly don't." The nurse bit her lip and Blood's eyes lingered.

"Well, one may arrive in due course," he said, scraping back his chair to stand. "Thank you, Nurse Farthing. If we have any more questions, we know where to find you."

"Of course." She stood and her smile felt like a warm blanket on a cold day. As she left the room, she cast a last look over her shoulder that caused his mind to go blank again.

Inspector Bridger chuckled. "Do you always have that effect on the ladies?"

"I don't know what you are talking about, Inspector?" he snapped, a little more brusquely than he had intended.
The shot found its mark and the inspector's face fell.

"Time to question the rest of the staff," Blood barked.

# Chapter 5

They found the head gardener, Wright, in a large, earthy-smelling potting shed, elbow deep in dirt and pots. He looked to be about sixty and had not missed too many meals. As they entered, he looked up but continued his work.

"Chief Inspector Blood and Inspector Bridger." Blood flashed some credentials, but the gardener didn't look. "We need to ask some questions about the missing dog."

"Oh aye. Ask away," croaked the man.

The scent of fresh mint punched the air as the gardener pushed a sprig into a pot, his hands scratched and dirty.

"You were in charge of exercising the dog as I understand it."

Wright nodded.

"Why was this task not assigned to a servant with less authority?" asked Blood.

Wright stuck a hand shovel into the dark potting soil and pushed back his cap to wipe his brow. "You obviously don't know her ladyship very well," he began. "She didn't trust any of the lower staff, said they were too young and irresponsible. Told me it was a matter of trust." He scrunched his large, pore filled nose. "It's an honor, she said." A cross between a growl and a grunt erupted from the gardener.

Living in the city, Blood was not a gardener, but he could appreciate the smell of freshly dug earth as well as the next man. "And how long had you been exercising the animal?"

"Nigh on five years." Wright delivered the news as if he were speaking of a prison sentence.

Blood had difficulty hiding a grin and exchanged a look with Inspector Bridger.

"I take it you were not fond of the dog."

The gardener made a sound that was almost a laugh. "Not fond of the pipsqueak? No! I like real dogs. Dogs that serve some purpose not spoiled little beggars that do nothing but yap all day long."

Inspector Bridger stepped forward. "Did you hate the dog enough to hurt it?"

Wright stepped back, eyes wounded. "Come on, now. What are you accusing me of? I may not have liked the little rat, but I did my job. I never hurt the stupid animal." He put down the shovel and laid his palms on the table. "But I would be lying if I said I missed the daft thing."

Now that the man was on the defensive, Blood thought it was time to hear the details of the day the dog disappeared.

"Run me through that day. Was it any different from any other?"

"The day before, I had left the dopey thing running around in circles after our walk and gone to find a tool. When I came back, I couldn't find her for a few minutes, which is not unusual.

"I called out and after a while she came running from those trees, yonder." He pointed with the shovel and soil cascaded to the wooden floor. "I didn't think much of it. Then the next day, the same thing happened, and I called her, but this time she didn't come running. I walked over to the trees but she was nowhere to be found. That's when I started to panic. Thought I'd lose my job for sure. I looked for a couple of hours then ran in to tell the master. He was most understanding. He's a good man he is."

Blood glanced through the grimy window that looked out onto the trees. "And you saw no strangers on the grounds that day?"

"No sir. But that doesn't mean there weren't any. I'm tucked away over here when I'm in this shed." Wright pulled his sagging trousers up.

The trees were about twenty feet from the gardener's nursery. Out of the other window Blood could see rows of greenhouses. "But she had never wandered off before without coming back when you called?" he asked.

"Never." The old gardener twitched his large nose.

This had proven to be a bit of a dead end. Blood supposed they could look for a trail in the woods but if the animal went there as part of her usual routine how would they distinguish one trail from another?

"I have been told she barks a lot. Did you hear her barking before you went to find her?" he asked.

The gardener raised a grubby hand to grip his mouth, as his eyes narrowed in concentration. "Now that you mention it, I don't think I did. But if a stranger tried to take her, she would have barked up a storm and tried to bite the fellow." He fixed Blood with a rheumy eye. "Perhaps they used chloroform."

Blood tried to imagine a stranger gaining access to the estate, luring the dog and then sedating her. "That is a possibility," he conceded. "Thank you, Wright. If I have any more questions, I know where to find you."

They moved to the door and the gardener followed them. "What's a chief inspector doing looking into the disappearance of a dog, if you don't mind me asking."

"I do," replied Blood, straightening his hat. "Let's just say your master is an influential man."

The old man nodded, the twist of his mouth betraying his dissatisfaction with the answer.

Ж

The pair of policemen went back to the large, modern kitchens. The housekeeper, Mrs. Martin, ran a tight ship and the servants merely flicked their eyes at the two strangers before returning to their assigned tasks.

Mrs. Martin allowed them to conduct the servant interviews in her spotless sitting room and they questioned a line of nervous maids and gangly footmen without discovering any information that was helpful.

The housekeeper returned with a tea tray and plate of biscuits and sat in one of the chairs.

"How long have you worked here," began Chief Inspector Blood, biting into a buttery biscuit that melted on his tongue.

"Thirty years," she replied, checking the back of her gray hair with a deeply veined hand. "Can you believe I started as a lowly housemaid and worked my way up. I've seen many people come and go."

"I bet you've seen some changes," commented Inspector Bridger.

"Oh my, yes," said Mrs. Martin. "And not all of them good!" She chuckled and her laugh was like a bubble that sat in her throat.

"Did you have anything to do with her ladyship's dog?" asked Blood, taking another biscuit.

"No. Lady Monroe-Spencer mostly takes care of—" she stopped and covered her mouth with her hand. "Oh! I keep forgetting the dog is gone. Her ladyship took care of her except for the exercising which is done by Wright the gardener. And her food which is brought up by a maid twice a day."

"Have you noticed anything out of the ordinary recently?" asked Blood, replacing his cup and saucer on the table. The tea was excellent too.

"Well, the maid, Lucy Starks, keeps staring at Robby Farnton, the second footman as if she's never seen him before, but that's probably not the kind of thing you are interested in." There was a twinkle in her eye. Blood had been wrong—she could smile, and it transformed her face. He had the feeling it was a rare sight.

She tapped her chin. "I really can't. Everything has been as it usually is.

A clock struck the hour. "Now, if you will excuse me, I have things to attend to," she said. "Unless there is anything else?"

"There is one thing. Nurse Farthing said her cat has gone missing,"

The efficient housekeeper put her hand to her throat. "Missing? Oh no! Why didn't she say? Two animals missing. Do you think someone has taken them?" Her eyes bulged. "Do you think they are dead?"

"The fact that both animals are missing does lead me to think they may have been taken, yes. But as to their…condition. Let's not jump to any conclusions just yet."

A knock on the parlor door interrupted them and seeing a maid, Mrs. Martin stood up and whispered something to the girl's question. Turning she explained, "A minor emergency, Chief Inspector. Will that be all?"

"Yes, I think we're done. Please don't mention the missing cat to anyone. Thank you for your time and for the tea. Can you send the cook in to see me?" He checked his watch. "Or is it too close to dinner?"

Mrs. Martin opened the door. "I think Mrs. Green can spare five minutes. The scullery maid can get things ready."

"What are your thoughts so far," asked Inspector Bridger as the housekeeper left, leaving them alone in the room.

"The fact that the gardener couldn't find the dog for a bit the day before leads me to believe this was planned, not random, and therefore the minister may have good reason to be worried. I would guess that the cat was in the wrong place at the wrong time."

After a light knock, a portly woman with a gray bun, hidden under a white cap, slipped into the room. She wore an immaculately clean apron and bore a smudge of flour on one cheek.

"Mrs. Green?" asked Blood. "Please take a seat."

The cook's eyes were troubled. "I'm not sure that I can help in any way," she began, her gaze darting around the room.

"Let me be the judge of that," Blood began in a gentle tone. "I am interested in anything out of the ordinary that may have happened the day her Ladyship's dog disappeared.

The cook gripped her chin, then poked the air with a finger. "Mrs. Harris, Lady De Courcy's cook came over for tea. We've known each other since we were knee high."

"Is that unusual?" asked Blood.

"No, she comes a couple of times a year and I go there from time to time, but you asked about things that happened that day." She brushed the flour from her rosy cheek.

Blood squeezed his mouth with his fingers. Nothing suspicious there.

"Oh!" continued the cook. "She was late. She often is but she was fifteen minutes late this time. I asked her why and she said a lot of words that didn't tell me anything. I didn't push it."

Now that was something. He made a note to talk to the De Courcy's cook.

"And what did you two talk about?"

"The usual, varicose veins, lumbago, the shocking price of beef." She folded her arms across her ample chest. "She was in a right hurry to go though."

"Did she say why?"

"Just some song and dance about profiteroles. I can make those in my sleep." Her mouth flattened and he realized she was wearing dentures.

Blood looked at Bridger to see if he had any questions. He shook his head.

"Thank you, Mrs. Green. That will be all for now."

She smiled the kind of smile you might give your dentist when you arrive and hurried out of the room.

"There's at least one woman you had no effect on," said Bridger, his face betraying that he spoke, in spite of worrying that he would incur the chief inspector's wrath.

Blood replaced his hat, pulling it down with his hand. Bridger's face fell until Blood's face split into a grin. "You've got me there, Inspector."

# Chapter 6

Blood and Inspector Bridger had strolled into the village to get some dinner at the local pub, *The Dog and Whistle*.

"What are you thinking?" asked Inspector Bridger over a steaming steak and kidney pie.

"About the dog?" said Blood, his mind elsewhere as he dipped his fork into an Irish stew.

The right side of the inspector's mouth curled into a smile. "Yes, the dog. What else would I mean?"

The inspector was spot on. Blood had allowed a sad pair of oval eyes, framed with dark lashes to distract him. He cleared his throat.

"I met my wife on the job," said Bridger with a cheeky grin. "She was a witness in a robbery."

Blood frowned at his companion, pretending to be affronted. "Now, now inspector. The beautiful nurse may prove diverting but don't let your imagination run away with you."

"My apologies, sir. I thought I saw a mutual—never mind." He filled his mouth with the light brown, flaky crust.

Blood cleared his throat. "A dog and a cat go missing. No one sees any strangers or hears anything. It's not much to go on."

A group of rowdy regulars were yucking it up in a dark corner of the room.

"Perhaps we should question the other cook—the one who came to visit. Maybe she saw something as she was arriving or leaving." Inspector Bridger took a long pull on his beer.

"That is an idea. I'd also like to look into the jewel theft. It's nagging at me. We could ask about that at the same time." He glanced at his watch. "If we time it right, we can arrive after the dinner is served upstairs."

Inspector Bridger scraped his knife across the plate, wiping up the rich gravy. "Got time for pudding, sir?"

"Yes, I think so."

The inside of the pub was paneled in dark walnut that absorbed any sunlight that managed to penetrate the small windows. The whole interior was dark and smoky.

"Apple pie or apricot crumble?" Bridger asked as he headed back to the bar.

"Apricot, thanks."

He looked around at the customers as he finished off the stew. Mostly working men spending all their wages on beer. There were one or two younger women, obviously out on the town with their young men. They looked happy. He thought back to the dimple in the nurse's smile. Perhaps he *was* ready to settle down.

"Here you go!" said the inspector, placing a bowl of crumble, covered with thick yellow custard, in front of Blood.

"Thank you."

As Bridger dug into the pie, he said, "If you don't mind me saying so, sir, I was surprised how young you are for a chief inspector."

Blood slid his eyes to Bridger over the top of his glass. "I suppose I am. I don't spend too much time thinking about it."

"How is it up at HQ?" Bridger was sporting a fine hops mustache and wiped his hand across his top lip.

"Lots of red tape," replied Blood with a smile.

"I can only imagine," said Bridger. "I've been a policeman for almost twenty-five years now. It's an interesting job. Every day different."

"Do you have a family?" asked Blood.

"Oh yes! The wife and I have three boys. The oldest two are adults now. One is a copper. The other a car mechanic. The youngest is still at school."

"How does your wife feel about your work?"

"Depends. She'd like me home at a regular time for dinner more often but on the whole she doesn't mind. I bounce ideas off her when I'm stumped about a case I'm working on. Full of common sense my wife, is. Many's the time she has said something that has led me in the right direction."

This was a thought that had never crossed Blood's mind—collaboration on cases with a wife. A trusted partner.

"How about you, Chief Inspector? Ever thought of marriage?"

"Not until very recently, no. I always thought it would be too hard on a wife. The travel, the long, irregular hours." He looked at the inspector. "But your perspective has me thinking along different lines."

Bridger leaned back in his chair, hands crossed over his ample stomach. "If I didn't have Enid to go home to—well, it's a steadying influence in a man's life," he said. "When the day has been hard, she's there to comfort me. Nothing like it."

Finishing the crumble, Blood laid down his spoon and wiped his mouth. "And the boys. Do you get to spend enough time with them?"

Bridger wagged his finger. "They are my pride and joy, sir. My life's work really. Anyone can do this job when I'm retired but no one can be the father to my boys. I wasn't always able to be there for them, but can any father? We all have to work, don't we? I was there enough. I love my boys and I know they love me."

Except for the weekly dinner at his mother's, Blood had no one.

"Lookey who's here," said Bridger, rousing Blood from his reverie. "If it isn't your nurse."

As Blood looked up, he spat out, "Not *my* nurse, Bridger."

"Sorry, sir. Forgive my familiarity. I can't help myself sometimes." He chuckled, not sounding the least sorry.

A ray of the setting sun was shining on Nurse Farthing's coppery hair that had been freed from the cap, forming a frame of curls around her pretty face.

Bridger waved his hand to get her attention. When her eyes landed on Blood, her whole face lit up.

His pulse ticked up as he saw that she had trouble tearing her gaze away from his to direct her words to his companion. "Inspector Bridger. How nice to see you here."

Blood jumped up almost spilling his drink "Can we get you something?"

"I'd like that," she said. "Gin and tonic please."

He strode over to the bar, aware that his heart was beating a strange tattoo.

When he returned to the battered table, the inspector and the nurse were laughing about something.

"Here you go." He placed the small glass on the table and sat next to Nurse Farthing.

"I don't suppose you have found out anything about my cat?" The smile had fallen and her forehead was creased with worry.

He felt an urge to reach out and touch her hand. "Not yet. We'll contact you as soon as we hear anything." He picked up his glass and swirled the amber liquid around.

"You mentioned something about a jewel theft a few miles away. We were wondering about it. Can you tell us anything?" Blood asked.

Nurse Farthing frowned. "Really? What on earth would that have to do with this?"

"I'm not saying it does. You mentioned it and the story peeked out interest."

"Well, I don't know much. Lady De Courcy had a special diamond necklace made for her sixtieth birthday which was in the spring. She gave it to her lady's maid to clean before a special dinner with the ambassador to France. As I heard it, the maid put it in a cupboard, planning to polish it when she had a minute but when she went back it was gone. She was fired."

*I don't doubt it.* "When was that?"

"Saturday, I believe."

*Interesting timing.*

Nurse Farthing checked her watch. "Are you expecting someone?" Blood asked.

"I'm meeting my sister, but I'm early." She smiled at him, and for a moment, the other people in the room faded away.

"Do you enjoy your job, Nurse Farthing?" he asked.

Bridger cleared his throat and mumbled something about settling the bill.

"I worked in a hospital before this. On my feet all day, busy all the time. Too many patients. This job is a welcome relief."

"You think you'll stay?"

"Not long term. Her ladyship is quite young still, but certainly for a couple more years. Then I'd like to go abroad and do some nursing in Africa."

"Really? What led to your interest in that?"

"I have a friend, a doctor, who leads humanitarian trips over there. He's been asking me to go for a while now."

Blood huffed and his mood took a downturn. *Of course she'd have an admirer.* The sun suddenly looked a little less bright.

She took a sip from her glass unaware that she had just trampled all over any hopes he might have entertained about getting to know her better. "What about you, Chief Inspector? Do you like fighting crime?"

"I find it fulfilling as I am sure nursing is for you," he began. "I can't imagine doing anything else."

"What are your ambitions?" She tipped her head and the long, red curls fell over her shoulder.

"I don't really know. I just keep working and trying for promotions when they come." He grasped his glass with both hands.

"Well, do you want to be the commissioner one day?"

Blood chortled. "I can honestly say I have not thought about it." His face relaxed into a deep smile and he saw a change in her eyes.

"But why not?" She laughed and the delightful sound was like fairies celebrating.

Bridger returned and standing behind Nurse Farthing, tapped his watch.

"Time for me to go," Blood said, pushing back his chair.

Nurse Farthing held out her hand. "Thanks for the drink." He took her warm hand and it fit in his like the proverbial glove.

"I want to assure you that we *are* looking for your cat too," he said, warmly.

She looked up at him through her lashes. "I appreciate that, Chief Inspector."

# *Chapter 7*

Blood took an instant dislike to the De Courcy's cook.

"Why are you here?" she rasped, her voice dry and crackly. "This is the only time of day I have to myself."

This was a part of the job he did not like—ingratiating himself to irascible witnesses or victims.

Whereas the kitchen at Wentworth Park was all modern efficiency, the kitchen here was like stepping back in time and it was clear that the maids were in awe of the bad-tempered cook.

"We are looking into the disappearance of Lady Monroe-Spencer's dog, and I am interested in the fact that there was a recent theft here."

The old woman shifted in her seat and looked at the floor, shaking her head and muttering. "What on earth has that got to do with anything?"

Blood took a breath to dig deep for patience. "Maybe nothing, but I won't know until I have investigated the theft."

Avoiding his eye, the cook tapped her rough fingers on the table. "I'm sure I don't know anything about it," she mumbled. "Why ask me?"

Bridger took over. "Well, the lady's maid was fired we understand, and the housekeeper is at her sister's and was also not here the day of the crime. As the next most senior member of the downstairs kitchen staff, we came to you first."

*Flattery. Good job, Bridger.*

Mrs. Fletcher, the De Courcy's cook, stretched her neck. "Yes, well, you've got that right. Nothing goes on down here that I don't know about."

"So, the theft?" Blood asked, notebook to the ready.

"Not much to tell. Miss Fairchild, the lady's maid, brought the necklace down for polishing and put it in that cupboard which she locked with a key." She pointed to a respectable, oak cupboard in the corner of the room. "When she went to get it later it was gone. End of story."

"What do you think happened to it?" Blood asked her.

The cook's beady, dark eyes narrowed. "I reckon she hid it somewhere with plans to sell it later. It was too much of a temptation."

"What did she say when questioned?"

"She acted the innocent. Pretended to be astounded that it had disappeared and burst into tears. Over-acting if you ask me."

"Was she arrested?" He would call the officer in charge after their visit to find out the official version.

"Should ha'been. I think they took her in for questioning and then let her go."

"Did they question you?"

"Aye. But I didn't have much to tell them. I had a big dinner that day what with the ambassador coming and was run off my feet. I didn't notice nothing."

Bridger wandered over to the cupboard and inspected the lock, jiggling the door up and down.

"Were there any other suspects?" he asked.

"They questioned the gardeners and all the staff but came up empty." She crossed her arms.

"Well, it's early days yet. I suspect they have leads they are following up. Thank you for your time." He stood and tipped his hat to her.

The old biddy followed them to the basement door. As Bridger opened it and Blood reached the top of the stone steps, he caught sight of a figure in the distance that hopped behind a tree. "Expecting anyone?" Blood asked turning back to the cook.

Her face compressed like a bull frog. "Nope!" She slammed the door, leaving Blood and Inspector Bridger aghast.

"Did you see someone?" Blood asked Bridger.

"I certainly did, sir. I'd bet good money that it was the gardener from Wentworth Park."

# Chapter 8

Blood ran like an Olympic sprinter in the direction he had seen the figure, with Bridger bringing up the rear.

"Hello, Mr. Wright," he gasped as he slid around an ancient oak to find the gardener, head back, eyes closed. He snapped them open. "What are you doing here?" continued Blood as Bridger caught up, gasping and clutching his stomach.

"Hello, Chief Inspector. I was checking the bark of this tree to make sure it's healthy."

Blood gulped in some air before asking, "But why are you here, at the De Courcy estate?"

"Oh, well, I'm here to see the cook, Mrs. Fletcher. We are, um, stepping out together, she and I."

Blood had no idea what he had expected the irascible old gardener to say but that was not it. He pushed back his hat and chuckled.

"Is it so unthinkable that someone would want to be with me, Chief Inspector?" growled Wright, his jaw set firm.

Blood tried to rearrange his features. "Of course not, Mr. Wright. My apologies."

"Can I go?" Wright's face had descended into a scowl that it might never recover from.

Blood had definitely seen the gardener rush to avoid detection. "I do not believe your story about the bark of the tree. Why did you try to hide from us?"

"Your reaction to why I am here should answer that question, Chief Inspector. No one likes humiliation." The gardener rubbed his bulbous nose.

He had a point.

"Of course. Enjoy your evening."

As Blood watched Wright amble down the path toward the basement kitchen, he chewed the inside of his cheek. His gut was telling him something was not right.

"Do you believe him?" asked Bridger, whose breathing had finally resumed its normal pattern.

"Do you?" countered Blood.

Bridger scratched his head. "There's something shifty about that fellow. I don't trust him, but I can't say why."

"I feel the same. How about we do a little snooping while he is safely out of the way?"

"Splendid idea, Chief Inspector."

Ж

They placed a call to Wentworth Park to discover Wright's address.

"Oh, Chief Inspector! We are all at sixes and sevens!" gulped the housekeeper.

"Whatever for?" asked Blood, his spine beginning to tingle with apprehension.

"It's Nurse Farthing. She has not returned to give the mistress her nightly medications."

Blood felt a jolt pass through him. "Have you talked to her sister?"

"Yes. She said they parted ways just outside the pub around seven. She's worried sick."

"Which way would she have walked back?" He was drumming the top of the telephone.

"There's a short cut across the back of the estate, goes right past Wright's cottage."

Having discovered the location of the cottage Blood exited the phone booth.

"What's wrong?" asked Bridger.

"What do you mean?" asked Blood, his eyes darting to the inspector.

"You look like you've just been told your grandma died."

"The nurse is missing." The amount of fear and concern that was fighting for attention in his chest showed him that he felt more than a passing interest in the woman. "She walked home from the village through the estate, near the gardener's cottage." He twisted his neck. "Let's go, man!"

Though it was late summer, dusk had fallen and the cottage had no lights. Blood could feel his pulse in his ears as he picked his way around the exterior of the cottage, Bridger at his heels keeping watch for the return of the gardener. He peered in the windows but could see nothing. Without a warrant they could not enter the premises.

As they searched the back of the property a second time, Blood felt his shoe slide into something soft and looking down saw that he had stepped in some fresh dog waste.

"Bridger! Look!"

The inspector dropped his gaze and his mouth pulled down into a frown. "Eww. You'd better wipe that on the grass, sir."

"Do you remember the gardener saying he had a dog?"

Bridger locked eyes with his boss. "No. He said he liked 'real' dogs, but he did not say he had one, as I recall. Do you suppose we've found our dog-napper?"

Blood decided it was time to make some noise. He whistled loudly. From inside they heard a yapping bark. Blood slapped his thigh. "Well, I never."

He rattled the back doorknob which was shut tight. Above the barking he heard a noise and rattled the door handle again, leaning his ear against the glass.

It was a person.

Taking a rock from the flower bed he tapped the glass until it broke and reached in to unlatch the door. Standing in the small kitchen he could hear someone yelling for help above the incessant dog yapping.

It was a woman.

Following the sound, the two men rushed through the cottage and came to a room that was locked.

"Hello!" cried Blood.

"Chief Inspector!" cried the muffled voice of the nurse as the dog lost its mind. "He tied me up and locked the door."

With one shove of the shoulder, Blood broke the lock to find the nurse tied to a chair in the cupboard. She burst into tears upon seeing him and it took all his self-control not to gather her into his arms.

"Bridger, find me a knife!" The inspector ran to the kitchen and returned with an old paring knife. Blood grabbed it and sliced through the bonds that tied the nurse. She fell against his chest and he could feel her trembling.

"What happened?" he asked after a moment.

Nurse Farthing pushed herself up, tears tracking down her cheeks. "I was coming home from the pub. I often come this way if I'm running late." She sniffed and Blood found a handkerchief. "As I rounded the hill, I saw Wright out in his back garden and could hear barking. Barking I knew only too well. I stared and Wright saw me. I froze." She pushed a hand through the auburn curls and Blood wanted to touch them.

"He caught me, dragged me back to the cottage and tied me up, muttering the whole time, things I did not understand. I asked him why he had taken the dog, but he just gave a mirthless laugh and shoved me in the cupboard."

She lifted green eyes that were swimming in tears. "Then I heard him leave after closing the dog in another room."

Blood tipped his head and Bridger went to the room next door and released the tiny ball of fur who threw herself into the nurse's arms. As she stroked the frightened dog's head another animal strode into the room.

A cat.

"Sooty!"

# Chapter 9

Unlike the dog, the cat stalked in as if she had all the time in the world, examining the various people in the room, with her nose in the air. She lifted her silky tail and yawned.

Nurse Farthing pushed the dog into Blood's arms and rushed to pick up the aloof feline, burying her face in the cat's fur. Blood promptly handed the dog to Bridger who held it as if it were a hedgehog.

"Oh, Sooty! Are you alright?" the nurse cried. A deep rumble emanated from Sooty indicating that she was perfectly fine, but this did not stop the nurse from examining every inch of her.

"Look, we had better get you out of here," said Blood looking at his watch. "Wright could be back at any minute."

The young nurse lifted eyes that were angry as hornets.

"Bridger can take you back to the main house," Blood continued. "I'll need to stay here and wait for Wright to come back."

"But I want to give him a piece of my mind," declared Nurse Farthing, hands on hips. "Who kidnaps someone's pet? Can't I stay?"

Bridger's face twisted in disagreement behind her, and he shook his head.

"We need to get the animals back to the house," said Blood, repositioning his hat.

Indignation and fury shone from the nurse's face.

He relented. "But you can come back with Inspector Bridger—if you stay out of the way."

Behind her, Bridger's brow rose like Tower Bridge. Blood ignored it. "Hurry now!"

As they sped away in the darkness, Blood walked back through the dwelling, into the kitchen. On the table lay some tools and a cloth bag. His eyes swept the rest of the room, seeing nothing else of interest.

He carefully closed the front door and settled behind an obliging bush. He considered the events of the long day and as he did, certain things began to emerge from the fog of confusion.

Quicker than he thought possible, he heard a rustle behind him. The full moon gave enough light for him to make out Bridger and Nurse Farthing. He whistled low and the pair crouched down beside him. Nurse Farthing misjudged the space and bumped his arm with her shoulder which he found was not an unpleasant sensation.

Quiet, in the dark, he was aware of every breath she took.

Owls and bats swooped and darted, bent on their next meal. Clouds periodically covered the clear moon, obstructing visibility. No words were spoken as tensions rose.

The click of the gate indicated the return of the unsuspecting kidnapper. With the element of surprise on their side, Blood shot out of his hiding place and grabbed the gardener by the collar.

"What the...?" cried the disoriented Wright.

Bridger shone a torch in his face, revealing a heavily wrinkled face scrunched in fear.

Blood tightened his grip. "I am arresting you in the name of the law."

On recognizing Blood's voice, Wright put up a struggle but when Bridger joined the fight he sank in defeat. Blood marched him into the small cottage and Bridger switched on the light. The bare bulb was harsh after the darkness, and everyone squinted.

"On what grounds have you accosted me in my own house?" spat out the gardener, his weathered jaw clenched.

"Come now, Mr. Wright. What kind of an idiot do you take me for?" Blood tipped his head and Bridger made to leave the room.

Wide-eyed, Wright's gaze followed the inspector, his face drenched with fear. "Where's he goin'? Do you have a warrant? I have rights!"

Inspector Bridger stopped. "We don't need a warrant because we heard a female inside calling for help."

Any color remaining in Wright's countenance vanished.

Bridger stopped. "Do you hear that?" he asked.

With hunted eyes, Wright gasped, "What?"

"Nothing," said Bridger.

Wright's head jerked as he realized that the house was quiet.

Too quiet.

# Chapter 10

"I must caution you that you have the right to remain silent," began Blood. "But if there is anything you want to say I would be happy to hear it."

The gardener closed his eyes as his head sank to his chest.

"Then I shall tell *you* a story," said Blood. "You need not comment at this point but later, down the station, you may want to give a statement."

This comment did not provoke the defeated Wright to engage.

"Until I saw you at the De Courcy's house I did not believe this crime had any connection to the theft of Lady De Courcy's jewels, but it was a lead that any good policeman would follow, if only to rule it out. The minute you darted to hide behind that tree, the lens I was looking at this case through, shifted. I do not believe in coincidences Mr. Wright."

The light above their heads flickered and buzzed distracting them for a moment.

"In addition, your presence there gave me a window of time to inspect the outside of *your* house. I had no intention of entering it at the beginning, but you were neglectful in tidying your lawn and I had the unfortunate occasion of stepping in some fresh dog waste. This caused me to ask myself a question. Why would a man with no dog have dog waste in his garden?"

Blood picked up one of the tools from the table. Wright lifted his head and froze as Blood handled the sharp object.

"Chief Inspector Blood whistled which set a dog barking," continued Bridger. He tapped his finger to his temple. "Clever."

"And it was not a 'proper' bark," said Blood, laying heavy emphasis on the word. "It was an annoying yappy bark, the kind of bark one might expect from a dog like Lady Monroe-Spencer's."

He replaced the tool and fingered the black cloth bag.

"On placing my ear to the door imagine my surprise when I heard someone crying for help. Here was my invitation to enter." He nodded to Wright who went to the door and opened it. Nurse Farthing stalked in, reminding Blood of her cat, and placed her hands on the table directly in front of Wright who shrank.

Her face was dark as thunder.

"Crikey!" said the restrained man. "I would never have hurt you, Nurse Farthing. I just couldn't take the risk. It was sheer bad luck that you came home this way."

Nurse Farthing rubbed her sore wrists. "You did hurt me." She pouted and Blood's heart skittered. "And what were you going to do with me?"

"Nothing. I swear!" gasped the old man who had aged ten years since returning home. "I was going to leave for the Continent and never look back."

Blood thought of the suitcase he had almost tripped over. He would bet it was full of clothes.

"Why did you take poor Mitzi in the first place? Why would you put the mistress through that? Were you going to blackmail her?" The questions poured from the distressed nurse's mouth like bullets from a gun.

"This was never about blackmail," explained Blood. "This was about diamonds the whole time."

The nurse looked at him with confusion as the light flickered again.

"Mr. Wright here and Mrs. Fletcher, Lady De Courcy's cook, began seeing each other. I posit that one day, Mrs. Fletcher mentioned the necklace that Lady De Courcy had and how much money it was worth which led to the formulation of a plan to steal the necklace and run away to the Continent. The plan was pretty straight forward. The cook would remove the necklace from the kitchen cupboard when it was brought down for cleaning and pass it to Mr. Wright as soon as possible."

He picked up a small eye glass from the table. "Wright would disassemble the jewels, removing the diamonds from their setting and then the pair of them would disappear into the night, never to return."

"That cupboard didn't have a very good lock and anyway, the cook probably had a key," said Bridger. "She chose a time when the kitchen was extra busy with the dinner for the ambassador. Who would suspect the cook in the middle of preparing an important meal?"

"Who indeed?" agreed Blood. "I imagine everything was going as planned until disaster struck. And this is where I had to guess. I theorized that the day Wright was relieving the necklace of its jewels he did *not* take Mitzi for her walk. Time was of the essence; everyone, including the police, was looking for the diamonds. He brought the dog here and her faithful friend—" He turned and gestured to Nurse Farthing. "—the good nurse's cat, followed. Cats are much more nimble than dogs and I can just see her walking on the table and knocking the gems to the floor."

Wright's bushy, white eyebrows danced a jig.

"If Mitzi is like most dogs, she would have been interested to see what fell and, for this story to make any sense, I think she swallowed the diamonds."

Nurse Farthing's hands flew to her face. "Yes! Mitzi eats anything. We have to be very careful."

"Perhaps you turned your back to make a cup of tea or something but when you turned back some of the jewels were gone. In your defense, you did not kill the animal to retrieve the diamonds, but you would have to wait for nature to take its course and you couldn't have that happening under Lady Monroe-Spencer's nose, so you had to keep the dog here and make up some story about her being kidnapped."

Bridger removed his hat and scratched his head. "By gum!"

"And as soon as the gems were recovered Mitzi would re-appear none the worse for wear."

"Diabolical, yet brilliant!" uttered the stunned nurse. "And I ruined everything by seeing you in the garden with the dog." She sank into one of the rickety kitchen chairs.

"After popping you in the cupboard, he must have panicked and rushed over to his sweetheart's to tell her what had happened and together, decide what they should do. That's when we saw him."

Wright didn't have to say that Blood's theory was correct. It was written all over his seasoned face.

"Bridger, run to the house and call for back up.

"Yessir!"

# *Chapter 11*

Had he really only arrived the day before? Even for him, this was a quick resolution to a crime.

Blood was on hold with Whitehall as they searched for Lord Monroe-Spencer and fatigue was hitting him like a strong wind. The adrenaline rush had long since passed and he was left to his own strength which was excessively low after being awake all night. He leaned heavily on the side of the telephone cabinet.

"Chief Inspector?" The sound of Lord Monroe-Spencer's bark woke him, and he sat straight as he filled in his lordship on the details of the crime.

"By Jove! Wright? I can hardly believe it," cried Lord Monroe-Spencer. "He's been with us since the year dot!"

"Temptation comes to all of us, my lord."

"So it would seem. I'm just relieved it has nothing to do with this blasted policy. Tremendous job, Blood. I will mention this to the Prime Minister, you can count on that."

"Thank you, my lord."

The line went dead, and Blood moved out of the cabinet to find Bridger, but Nurse Farthing blocked him, holding a cup of tea. She extended the drink to him. It was just what he needed.

"Thank you," he said with a tired smile, taking a sweet sip.

"It's the least I can do since you saved me. I am in your debt, Chief Inspector."

An idea popped into his weary brain and he put the cup down on a convenient credenza. "How about we settle that debt by your agreeing to come to dinner with me?"

The eyes that were on his, flashed like brandy on a crepe suzette and a smile bloomed across her creamy cheeks. "Chief Inspector Blood, are you asking me on a date?"

Her expression had already given him a resounding yes, filling him with a confidence he might have otherwise lacked.

He took a step forward.

Nurse Farthing chewed the inside of her cheek and looked up at him through dark lashes.

"Yes. Yes, I am." He noticed a faint sprinkle of freckles across her nose and wondered why he hadn't noticed them before.

"Isn't it against the rules?" She pushed the auburn curls back over her shoulder and he itched to touch them.

"Only if you are a victim or a suspect in an ongoing crime," he murmured. "And this case is now closed."

She stepped closer and his breath caught. She was close enough to kiss. "Well, in that case…"

Their lips met in the lightest touch, sending electricity coursing through his veins. He reached for her fingers.

He hoped this was going to be the beginning of a very happy ending.

*The End*

I hope you enjoyed this cozy mystery novella, *Mystery at Wentworth Park*, and learned more about Chief Inspector Blood. For those who have read my Dodo Dorchester Mystery series you will know that Chief Inspector Blood featured in book one, *Murder at Farrington Hall* and in book three, *Murder at the Races*. If you are curious how I came up with the name Chief Inspector Blood send me a note and I will let you know.

Interested in a free prequel to the Dodo Dorchester Mystery series?

Go to https://dl.bookfunnel.com/997vvive24 to download *Mystery at the Derby*.

Book *1* of the series, *Murder at Farrington Hall* is available on Amazon.

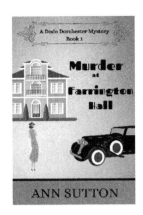

https://amzn.to/31WujyS

*"Dodo is invited to a weekend party at Farrington Hall. She and her sister are plunged into sleuthing when a murder occurs. Can she solve the crime before Scotland Yard's finest?"*

Book *2* of the series, *Murder is Fashionable* is available on Amazon.

https://amzn.to/2HBshwT

*"Stylish Dodo Dorchester is a well-known patron of fashion. Hired by the famous Renee Dubois to support her line of French designs, she travels between Paris and London frequently. Arriving for the showing of the Spring 1923 collection, Dodo is thrust into her role as an amateur detective when one of the fashion models is murdered. Working under the radar of the French DCJP Inspector Roget, she follows clues to solve the crime. Will the murderer prove to be the man she has fallen for?"*

Book *3* of the series, *Murder at the Races* is available on Amazon.

https://amzn.to/2QIdYKM

*"It is royal race day at Ascot, 1923. Lady Dorothea Dorchester, Dodo, has been invited by her childhood friend, Charlie, to an exclusive party in a private box with the added incentive of meeting the King and Queen. Charlie appears to be interested in something more than friendship when a murder interferes with his plans. The victim is one of the guests from the box and Dodo cannot resist poking around. When Chief Inspector Blood of Scotland Yard is assigned to the case, sparks fly between them again. The chief inspector and Dodo have worked together on a case before and he welcomes her assistance with the prickly upper-class suspects. But where does this leave poor Charlie?*
*Dodo eagerly works on solving the murder which may have its roots in the distant past. Can she find the killer before they strike again?"*

Book 4 of the series, *Murder on the Moors* is available on Amazon.

https://amzn.to/38SDX8d

**When you just want to run away and nurse your broken heart but murder comes knocking.**

*"Lady Dorothea Dorchester, Dodo, flees to her cousins' estate in Dartmoor in search of peace and relaxation after her devastating break-up with Charlie and the awkward attraction to Chief Inspector Blood that caused it. Horrified to learn that the arch-nemesis from her schooldays, Veronica Shufflebottom, has been invited, Dodo prepares for disappointment. However, all that pales when one of the guests disappears after a ramble on the foggy moors. Presumed dead, Dodo attempts to contact the local police to report the disappearance only to find that someone has tampered with the ancient phone. The infamous moor fog is too thick for safe travel and the guests are therefore stranded.*
*Can Dodo solve the case without the help of the police before the fog lifts?"*

Book 5 of the series, *Murder in Limehouse* is available on Amazon.

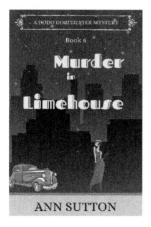

https://amzn.to/3pw2wzQ

**Aristocratic star she may be, but when her new love's sister is implicated in a murder, Dodo Dorchester rolls up her designer sleeves and plunges into the slums of London.**

*Dodo is back from the moors of Devon and diving into fashion business for the House of Dubois with one of the most celebrated department stores in England, while she waits for a call from Rupert Danforth, her newest love interest.*
*Curiously, the buyer she met with at the store, is murdered that night in the slums of Limehouse. It is only of passing interest because Dodo has no real connection to the crime. Besides, pursuing the promising relationship that began in Devon is a much higher priority.*

*However, fate has a different plan. Rupert's sister, Beatrice, is arrested for the murder of the very woman Dodo conducted business with at the fashionable store. Now she must solve the crime to protect the man she is fast falling in love with.*

*Can she do it before Beatrice is sent to trial?*


Book *6* of the series, *Murder on Christmas Eve,* is available on Amazon.

**Dodo is invited to meet Rupert's family for Christmas. What could possibly go wrong?**

*Fresh off the trauma of her last case, Dodo is relieved when Rupert suggests spending Christmas with his family at Knightsbrooke Priory.*
*The week begins with such promise until Rupert's grandmother, Adelaide, dies in the middle of their Christmas Eve dinner. She is ninety-five years old and the whole family considers it an untimely natural death, but something seems off to Dodo who uses the moment of shock to take a quick inventory of the body. Certain clues bring her to draw the conclusion that Adelaide has been murdered, but this news is not taken well.*
*With multiple family skeletons set rattling in the closets, the festive week of celebrations goes rapidly downhill and Dodo fears that Rupert's family will not forgive her meddling. Can she solve the case and win back their approval?*

For more information about the series go to my website at
www.annsuttonauthor.com and subscribe to my newsletter.

You can also follow me on Facebook at:
https://www.facebook.com/annsuttonauthor

# About the Author

Agatha Christie plunged me into the fabulous world of reading when I was 10. I was never the same. I read every one of her books I could lay my hands on. Mysteries remain my favorite genre to this day - so it was only natural that I would eventually write my own.

Born and raised in England, writing fiction about my homeland keeps me connected.

After finishing my degree in French and Education and raising my family, writing has become a favorite hobby.

I hope that Dame Agatha would enjoy Dodo Dorchester at much as I do.

# *Acknowledgements*

I would like to thank all those who have read my books, write reviews and provide suggestions as you continue to inspire.

Printed in Great Britain
by Amazon

40928980R00046